THE BOXCAR CHILDREN®

BY
GERTRUDE CHANDLER WARNER

BENNY UNCOVERS A MYSTERY

BOOK 19

ILLUSTRATED BY
DAVID CUNNINGHAM

ALBERT WHITMAN & COMPANY
CHICAGO, ILLINOIS

Miss Warner wishes
to thank everyone
who helped in any way
on this book

Cover art by Charles Tang
Interior illustrations by David Cunningham

Visit the Boxcar Children online at www.boxcarchildren.com.
For more information about Albert Whitman & Company,
visit our website at www.albertwhitman.com.

Contents

CHAPTER | PAGE

1 No Lazy Days for Benny   9
2 Wanted: A Summer Job   19
3 The Aldens Make an Enemy   29
4 A Mysterious Shopper   40
5 The Hidden House   47
6 Who Wrote the Letters?   58
7 A New Puzzle   72
8 Henry's Adventure   86
9 Benny Has Ideas   101
10 Answers at Last   114

BENNY UNCOVERS
A MYSTERY

CHAPTER 1

No Lazy Days for Benny

It was a hot, lazy morning, that last day of July. Not a leaf stirred in the huge maple tree in the Alden front yard. Even the birds were still.

Henry Alden sat on the grass with his back against a tree trunk. He was holding a book he was supposed to read for college in the fall. But he didn't feel like reading.

His sister Jessie sat with her back against another tree, not moving. Violet was lying on the grass, propping her head up with her hands. She watched the big white clouds float slowly by in the bright blue sky.

"Well," said Henry. "I don't remember a day like this ever. I don't feel like doing anything."

"Neither do I," said Jessie without stirring. "I don't see how Benny can be playing ball."

"I'll tell you why we feel this way," Violet said suddenly. "Usually Grandfather plans a trip in the summer. We've been at the lighthouse or on a houseboat or riding in a caboose."

Just then Benny came through the hedge. He had been next door. He was wearing shorts and a shirt with short sleeves.

"See you later," Jeff Beach called after him, and Benny waved.

"How's the ballgame?" asked Jessie. "Quitting?"

"Whew! It's just too hot for me," Benny said. He sat down next to Jessie. He did not look very happy.

"Who won, Benny?" asked Henry.

"Nobody won," answered Benny. "Jeff and I were just playing catch."

Jessie laughed and said, "That isn't exciting enough for you, Ben, is it?"

"No, it isn't," agreed Benny. "But it's too lazy a day for much excitement." Then he added, "I have one piece of news. Sammy Beach has a job."

"He has!" exclaimed Jessie. "Where?"

"He's an errand boy at the hospital. He likes it and he's earning money. It sounded good when Jeff told me about it. Sammy's so busy he forgets about the heat . . ."

Just then the paperboy came into the driveway with the Greenfield paper.

"Catch!" he called as he tossed the paper into the circle where the Aldens sat.

After the paperboy had gone on his way, Henry slowly unfolded the newspaper. He said, "I suppose somebody ought to take the paper into Grandfather. I'm too lazy to move."

"I'll do it in a minute," said Violet.

Benny looked at his brother and sisters. They were just sitting there, not talking, not moving.

Aldens never acted this way! Benny had to do something. "You know what I think?" he asked. "I think we ought to go to work."

"Work?" repeated Henry. "You mean get a summer job? Now?"

"Yes, that's just what I mean," replied Benny. "If Sammy Beach is working, we can, too. I want a real job, not just doing chores and mowing the lawn." He sat up straight. "I want to go to work in the morning and come home at five."

Jessie smiled at Benny. "Violet and I will be busy soon.   We're going to work at the park. Violet is going to teach painting, and I'm going to be a lifeguard at the pool."

"I forgot," Benny said. "That's good for you. But I want to do something now."

Henry looked at Benny. "You work in school, Ben. You're busy after school and on Saturdays. Why work in the summer?"

"Oh, I work my fingers to the bone all the time," Benny said without a smile, and he held up one arm to look at. It was a strong and healthy arm. And the hand had five perfectly good fingers.

The Aldens all laughed, for they knew Benny liked to be busy, playing or working. But Benny was serious about a summer job. "Hey, let's look in the paper for ads. We can job hunt without making a move. How's that, Henry?"

Benny opened the Greenfield paper and looked for the page which said "Help Wanted."

"Here we are," he said, folding back the paper. Then Benny laughed. "I wouldn't be very good for this one. 'Wanted, young person to sit two hours daily with invalid.' I know I couldn't be quiet that long."

"You're right about that," Jessie agreed.

Benny ran his finger down the ads. "Say!" he exclaimed. "Here's one for me after all. 'Wanted, someone for errands, some yard work. No driving necessary. Phone 222-1212.'"

Before anyone could stop him, Benny was on his feet and headed for the house. "Easy number to remember, just 222-1212," he called back.

"He really wants to work," said Henry. "I wonder if anyone will be home on a day like this to answer the phone?"

Inside the house Benny propped the paper by the phone and dialed the number. The phone rang five times before someone answered.

"Hello," said Benny. "Is this 222-1212? I'm calling about your ad in today's paper. My name is Benny Alden and I'd like the job."

A woman's voice said, "Benny Alden? Mr. James Alden's grandson? I'm sorry, but another boy just called and I promised him the job. Thank you for calling." And the phone clicked in Benny's ear.

Putting the phone down, Benny frowned. Who knew he was Mr. Alden's grandson, but wouldn't give a name or an address? Was it an older woman or had the voice just sounded that way? And had someone else really taken the job or didn't this person want an Alden to do the work?

Still feeling puzzled, Benny reported back to the others. "No luck," he said. "I guess you can't always get a job the first time you try."

Violet looked toward the porch and saw Grandfather Alden standing there, smiling at them. He loved to have his grandchildren make their own plans and carry them out. He only helped them if they needed him.

Now he put in a word. "Remember that Mrs. McGregor has a vacation. We'll have to be our own housekeepers while she's gone to Canada."

"Oh, yes, I know that," said Benny. "But that won't be too much to do."

Grandfather Alden laughed. Benny always wanted to be busy.

"Let's get back to the newspaper ads," said Benny. "Now where were we? Say, this may be it. 'Wanted, for the month of August only, sales clerk. Inquire at Furman's Department Store.' That sounds like something for you, Henry. You could do that."

"Well," Henry said. "That might be interesting. But that's just one job. What about you, Benny?"

"Nothing else here for me," Benny said and ran over to give Grandfather Alden the paper. When he came back to the others he said, "Maybe if Mr. Furman sees how much I want a job, he'll find something for me, too. Or maybe I can get a job at another store. I'll ask. Come on, Henry, let's go."

Jessie and Violet smiled at each other.

Benny was always like that. If he planned to do anything, he wanted to start at once.

Grandfather laughed, but Henry said, "You can't say a word, Grandfather. You are just like that yourself." And Mr. Alden had to agree.

"Yes, yes," he said, holding up his hand. "I think it's a fine plan. You'll both learn a lot, whatever you do. In fact, I'll be interested in learning about what's going on at Furman's Department Store. I've heard there are some changes planned there. Not everyone is happy about them."

Benny nodded. He didn't think any changes would make a difference to him and Henry. He said, "Let's go, Henry. Somebody else may get there ahead of us. I'd really like to work in a department store. I just hope I'm old enough. I'm sure you will be."

"OK," answered Henry, getting up and closing his book. "We'll see which of us the manager wants. Maybe he won't want either of us. Of course, Mr.

Furman knows us—for years and years. But he may want somebody older."

"Maybe he will, but I hope not," Benny said, starting toward the house.

The boys raced upstairs. They moved quickly, changing their clothes, brushing their hair. They forgot about the lazy summer day.

As the boys got ready Mr. Alden thought to himself, "When people are interested in something special, they don't notice how hot it is."

The boys got out their bikes. Henry called to Grandfather and the girls, "We'll probably be back soon. It would be pretty lucky to get a job on the first try."

"I don't think we'll be back," Benny put in. "I still feel lucky today. We may be working men in an hour or so. I'm ready to start right now."

"Come back for lunch or not, it's all right either way," said Jessie. "I'll be ready."

"Good luck," Violet called after them as the boys pedaled away.

CHAPTER 2

Wanted: A Summer Job

As they rode along, Benny said, "The girls are lucky. They already have jobs. They each have their own, but so far we just know of one job and there are two of us."

Henry asked, "What would you really like to do if you could do anything you wanted?"

"I like the idea of working in a store," Benny said. "I'd like to wait on customers. Maybe a hardware store would be the best place to work. Lots of people come in for tools and garden hoses and rakes. I could sell eggbeaters and cupcake tins and hammers and saws."

Benny smiled at the thought of all the interesting things there are in a hardware store.

"Well, why not go to the hardware store first, then?" asked Henry. "Maybe this will be your lucky day."

But Benny saw Tucker's Grocery Store. It was an old-fashioned store and Benny knew Mr. Tucker and his wife. "I'd like to work here, too," he told Henry. "I could make those fancy piles of apples and oranges in the window."

"What ideas you have, Ben," Henry said. "It's more likely you'd have to handle cartons of eggs. You would feel terrible if you broke any eggs."

"Maybe I wouldn't break any eggs," said Benny. "Mr. Tucker has known us for a long time. He'd give us jobs if he could."

So the boys parked their bikes in front of Tucker's Grocery Store and went inside.

"Well, hello, boys," said Mr. Tucker. "It's a hot day to go grocery shopping."

Henry looked around. "As a matter of fact," he said, "we aren't shopping for groceries at all. We're shopping for jobs."

Mr. Tucker sat down on a high stool. He exclaimed, "You're just too late! I wish you had come yesterday. I just hired a young man to help me out. I needed a helper who's strong to put things away. No matter how often I do it, there's more to be done. So I hired Tad Decker."

"Well, maybe he needs a job more than we do," said Henry.

"He does," said Mr. Tucker. "His father has lost his job, and Tad has to work. I'm sorry about you boys, though. I'd like to have a couple of Aldens work for me if I could. Try the hardware store. Maybe Mr. Green or Mr. Spencer has something."

"Thanks," said Henry and Benny together. "We'll go there next."

"Good luck," Mr. Tucker called.

When the boys had locked their bikes in front of the hardware store, they swung open the heavy door. They found the store empty. There was not a single customer in sight. Mr. Spencer and Mr. Green were leaning against a counter, talking in low tones to each other.

The boys knew the answer to their question before they asked it. The men shook their heads.

Mr. Spencer said, "As you can see, boys, our business is slow in the mornings. I'm sorry we have nothing for you."

"That's OK," said Benny. "Of course, we've had no experience."

"That's not the reason," replied Mr. Green. "We just don't need any more help now."

The boys said goodbye and left the store.

"Let's stop next door and see Mr. Shaw at the jewelry store," Henry said.

Shaw's Jewelry Store was a small shop with only one showroom. Mr. Shaw was in the back of the store, repairing a watch. As the boys opened the door, he pushed back the heavy blue curtain that hid his work table.

Mr. Shaw had a small magnifying glass over one eye. He pushed it up so that he could see the Aldens.

"It isn't often that you two come in," he said. "What can I do for you customers?"

"We aren't customers," said Benny. "We are looking for work."

"Sorry," said Mr. Shaw. "I haven't room for another person. I lock up the store when I go to lunch or do errands. Your best bet is Furman's."

When they were outside, Benny looked unhappy. "I didn't think it would be this hard to find a job. We should have gone to Furman's first. Someone else probably has that job by now."

"I don't think so," Henry said. "The paper just had the ad today. Let's try."

So the boys were off to Furman's, the biggest store in town. It was not like a city department store, but it had most of the things people in

Greenfield wanted to buy.

Furman's Department Store filled nearly a block in the business part of Greenfield. It had been a much smaller store when Mr. Furman's father had first begun it. Now it had new sections and two floors with many different departments.

Benny and Henry headed for the office as soon as they walked into the store. They knew where the office was, on a landing halfway up the stairs between the first and second floor.

Mr. Furman was in the office. It was a square room, something like a cage because the sides were built of open metal work. Mr. Furman could see almost all of the first floor counters when he looked out. Some people said he should make the store modern and put in glass walls. But Mr. Furman liked his office the way it was. It suited him.

He had seen Henry and Benny enter the store. He thought how big the boys were. He could remember when Benny had been so small that he came to the store with a note saying what he was to buy. The store people would make sure Benny had his purchases and the right change to take home.

Mr. Furman was surprised to see the Aldens pass the downstairs counters and come up the stairs to his private office. The worried look on his face changed to a smile.

Henry rapped on the door and Mr. Furman called out, "Come right in."

Henry was just going to explain the boys' errand

when Benny said in a rush, "We boys want to work until school starts. We saw the ad in the paper. Is the job still open?"

"Yes, it is," said Mr. Furman. "I've had trouble filling the job because it will only last from four to six weeks at the most. I need someone who can take the place of a salesperson when the regular worker goes on vacation."

Benny looked at Henry and smiled. The job sounded just right for Henry.

Mr. Furman went on. "There will be a lot of variety, but it can be hard to change from one department to another. I think it just might be right for Henry, though." He stopped and seemed to be thinking. "Yes, maybe you can do it, Henry. There will be some problems, I'm sure, but . . ."

When Mr. Furman did not say anything more, Henry said, "Well, Mr. Furman, I'd like to take the job. I only need to work until I go back to school. But it was really Benny's idea to go job hunting. He's the one who wants to be busy."

Benny and Henry looked at Mr. Furman and waited.

There was a long pause. Mr. Furman said thoughtfully, "Benny is a little young to work here full time. I'm afraid I have no work you would take, Benny."

"What do you mean?" asked Benny. "I'd take anything."

Mr. Furman laughed and asked, "You wouldn't want to be assistant delivery boy, would you?"

"Oh, yes, I would," said Benny.

Benny and Henry both smiled at Mr. Furman.

"Then it's settled," said Mr. Furman. "Come back after lunch and we'll handle the paperwork to get you hired. I'll introduce you to some of the department managers and salespeople. You'll be all set to start to work tomorrow morning."

The Aldens, still smiling, left Mr. Furman's office. Some of the people behind the counters called out hello to them. But one man carrying an electric fan scowled at the boys.

"Can't you see you're in the way?" he asked. "If you aren't buying something stand over there by the door, out of my path. This fan is heavy and my back hurts."

Benny started to say something, then changed his mind. If he was going to work at Furman's, he couldn't talk back to the other workers. He'd have to learn how to get along with them. And Benny felt sure he could do that.

But Henry remembered Grandfather's words about trouble at Furman's and wondered.

CHAPTER 3

The Aldens Make An Enemy

It was just after lunch when the two Aldens met the man who had scowled at them earlier that day.

"This is Mr. Fogg," Mr. Furman said. "Henry, you will be working with Mr. Fogg. He is the manager of the first floor. You can learn a lot from him."

Henry said, "How do you do, Mr. Fogg?" And Benny said, "Hi."

But there was no reply from Mr. Fogg.

Mr. Furman seemed not to notice. He went on, "Mr. Fogg is in charge of the small electrical appliances, such as steam irons and electric frypans. When we don't need you behind a counter, Henry, you will help Mr. Fogg stock the first floor."

"Stock the first floor?" asked Henry. He wanted to be sure he understood his job.

Mr. Furman said, "Yes, you will bring goods up from the basement. If Mrs. Lester wants boxes for jewelry, you will find them and take them up to her."

Henry nodded.

Mr. Fogg frowned and leaned forward. "I just don't approve of this at all," he said. "These two boys have no experience. They will be more trouble to me than they are worth. I don't need help like this."

The Alden boys could not believe their ears.

Mr. Furman tried to laugh. "Oh, come on, Mr. Fogg, give them a chance! I remember when you started your first day here. You had a lot to learn, too. When something wrong comes up, we can look into the matter. But I'm sure nothing will go wrong."

Mr. Fogg still did not smile.

Benny looked away from Mr. Fogg. He saw counters filled with things to sell. There were shoppers coming and going.

Benny said, "It must be wonderful to own a big store like this, Mr. Furman."

Mr. Furman glanced at Mr. Fogg and then shook his head. "I guess you boys don't know that I have sold the store. It was too much for me to handle, and I had a good offer. Of course, it's still called Furman's Department Store. And so far there haven't been any big changes."

Mr. Fogg was looking more and more gloomy. He muttered, "I suppose the new owner won't want me with my bad back. But I know the work."

Henry looked at Mr. Furman and asked, "But you're still in charge of the store, aren't you?"

"I'm just the store manager for the new owner, M.D. Squires. So far, I haven't met the new owner because he lives in New York. I've only met his lawyer. I'll say this, though, Mr. Squires has a good head for business."

"Oh?" Henry asked, wondering how this new owner could know about his store in Greenfield when he lived in New York.

"Yes, he's done a lot for the store already. When some new product appears, Mr. Squires knows if our store should carry it. Sometimes I've wanted to get something, but Mr. Squires writes and tells me to wait. More than once, I've learned that the product doesn't work well, or other stores in town couldn't sell the item at all."

"Mr. Squires must own other stores," guessed Benny.

"That may be it," said Mr. Furman. "It's hard to explain. But I have never known Mr. Squires to be wrong."

"I don't think it's so strange," Mr. Fogg put in.

"But no one listens to me."

"The new owner must be a fine person to work for," said Henry.

"Yes, indeed," said Mr. Furman. "Still, it isn't like the old days." Then he turned away from Mr. Fogg and led the boys down to the store basement. A man was unpacking goods to go on the counters upstairs.

Benny said, "I thought I knew this store very well, but I'm surprised. I was never down here before."

"You'll do a lot of your work here," Mr. Furman said. "There's always something to get or to take somewhere. Mr. Fogg can keep you busy all by himself."

Benny didn't like to hear this, but he said, "I never thought I would deliver things to the Greenfield people. This will be fun." Just then he saw Mr. Fogg on the stairs. His face was angry. Benny smiled, but Mr. Fogg did not return the smile. Instead, he turned to talk to the workman.

Mr. Furman led the boys up to the first floor again. Benny felt that Mr. Fogg was following them.

As they turned around a counter and headed toward the gift and glassware department, Benny heard Mr. Fogg's voice. He was speaking to someone Benny couldn't see.

"I don't know if those boys are good workers," Mr. Fogg was grumbling. "I just know that they're old man Alden's grandchildren. It would be nice to have someone like that in your family to help you get a job. Just like that, with no trouble at all."

Then Benny and Henry knew that they had an enemy. They had to pretend that they had not heard Mr. Fogg's words. But they were sure that he had meant them to hear.

Well, Benny thought, Grandfather had not helped them get their jobs. They had done it on their own. He followed Henry and Mr. Furman to another part of the store. The boys and Mr. Furman went from one counter to another. Each department had interesting people to meet, and there was so much for sale.

Mr. Furman introduced the boys to the head cashier, Mrs. Lippmann. "Just call me Toni," she said pleasantly. "Everyone calls me that."

Toni worked in a place where she had a fine view of the front door. She kept an eye on everything that was going on.

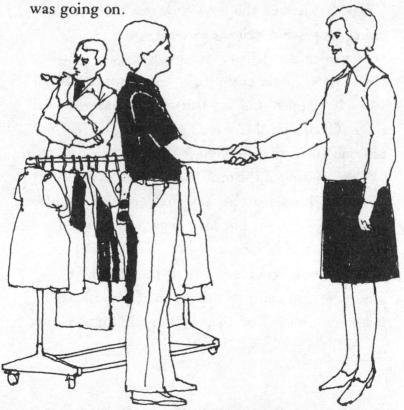

"I'll let Toni show you the rest of the store. Let me know if you need anything." Mr. Furman waved as he went back to his office.

Toni introduced the boys to Mrs. Lester, who was in charge of jewelry and glassware.

"You mustn't drop or lose anything here," Mrs. Lester explained. "Everything is so expensive." Then she showed the boys how much some small china figures and delicate teacups cost.

"I remember when Mr. Fogg began to work here," Mrs. Lester said softly. "He dropped a small vase. It chipped and we had to sell it at a special price. Of course, that was a long time ago. He won't tell you about that, though."

Toni continued the tour. Benny and Henry went past the shiny toasters and coffeemakers in Mr. Fogg's department, but Mr. Fogg paid no attention to Toni or the Aldens.

There were counters where things for sewing were sold and counters where combs and hairpins were on display. And there were socks for men and stockings for women—there was so much to see on the first floor alone.

Upstairs there were clothing departments for men, women, and children.

Toni led the boys back to the basement for the end of their tour. She said, "Now you know most of the store and this will mean more to you. Benny, you will pick up your orders here. Sometimes you will go out with the regular delivery man. But we give special service to a lot of our customers. You may have to deliver small purchases by yourself."

"That won't be hard. I can use my bike," said Benny.

Toni smiled. She showed the boys how the merchandise was arranged. There were aisles of boxes.

"Henry, the important thing for you to remember is that when you take stock upstairs, your list must match the list the department manager takes."

"I'll remember that. If the list says twelve boxes of candles, I'll be sure there are twelve."

"You won't get in trouble that way," Toni said. "But sometimes if a stockboy is in a hurry, he may think he has taken, say, six boxes of socks up to the boys' department. But there are only five. We have to account for every box."

"Thanks for warning me," Henry said.

"And don't leave things around," Toni went on. "I hate to say it, but every store has trouble with people who take things."

"You mean shoplifters?" Benny asked.

"Yes, even here in Greenfield. Of course, some people pick things up by mistake and just honestly forget to pay for them. A woman came in yesterday and paid for a box of notepaper she had taken by accident. She felt bad about it."

"There's a lot to think about in a store," Benny said thoughtfully.

"Well, boys, that's it," Toni said. "Mr. Furman has some papers for you to fill out. Come in by nine-thirty tomorrow morning. The store opens a half hour later, but you'll both have things to do."

At dinnertime at home, Henry told his sisters and his grandfather what had happened.

"Why are you so quiet, Ben?" asked Violet.

"It's just—just old man Fogg," Benny exploded. "Everything is fine except for him."

"Why, Benny, that doesn't sound like you at all," exclaimed Jessie.

"I can't help it. That man is going to make it hard for Henry and me. For some reason he doesn't like us, and he's not keeping that a secret."

Mr. Alden put down his coffee cup. "Well, Benny," he began, "you and Henry must do the best work you can. That is all anyone can ask of you. You will meet many people in the store, and it is your job to be as pleasant as possible."

"I'll try, but it won't be easy," Benny said. "Grandfather, Mr. Fogg didn't even give us a chance. He said right away that we had our jobs because we're Aldens."

"I see," said Grandfather. "I think you boys will learn a lot before your summer jobs are over."

CHAPTER 4

A Mysterious Shopper

Benny and Henry wondered how the first day at work would go.

That question was still on their minds as they entered the store the next morning at half past nine.

Toni was already there, sorting her change for the day.

"This is a good beginning. You're early. I'm glad to see you both," she said. "You'd better head downstairs, Benny. And Henry, you will be working with Mrs. Lester in the glassware and china department until the end of the week."

The boys started off. Mrs. Lester showed Henry how to make the sales reports. She told him a little about the different kinds of china and glass.

"We try to carry as many different pieces of glassware as we can, but sometimes a customer wants something we don't have. Then we send a special order." Mrs. Lester showed Henry where the special order forms were kept.

"Be sure to get an OK before you send out any orders," Mrs. Lester warned. "Mr. Fogg watches that. And there's one more thing," she said with a smile, "I want you and your brother to call me Doris."

Henry was just beginning to feel comfortable behind the counter when he noticed that suddenly the store was strangely quiet. Talking had stopped, and all the salespeople were looking in one direction.

Everyone was watching a little woman who had just entered the store.

Henry could not see anything unusual about the woman. She was far from stylish. Her hair was pulled back and pinned up in a bun. Her clothes were plain. They were not the kind that anyone would look at twice. She carried a worn handbag and a large, flowered shopping bag.

Henry couldn't decide how old the woman was. He caught Toni's eye. She came to his counter and said, "You must want to know who that is."

Henry nodded.

"She comes in every day. Her name is Maggie Douglas. She's always buying something. Sometimes two and three kinds of the same thing. Benny will be busy with her deliveries, I'm sure."

Henry and Toni watched the little woman climb the stairs to the second floor.

In a few minutes one of the salespeople from upstairs came over to Toni. "I have another 'Maggie story' for you. Miss Douglas just came to my counter and said she needed a blouse, a white blouse. When I asked her what size she needed, she said the size didn't matter. It only had to be a white blouse. Now, isn't that strange?"

Just then Mr. Fogg joined the group. He looked cross and asked, "That woman is in the store again, eh?"

The salesperson told him the story.

"You are foolish to sell a blouse to that woman," said Mr. Fogg. "We're going to have trouble with her sooner or later. I'm sure of it. Why didn't she ask for a blouse in her size? She'll bring it back to the store tomorrow and say it doesn't fit. Besides, all she has to do is walk into the store and all work stops."

With that, all the workers quickly left the counter. Henry was alone with Mr. Fogg standing right before him.

"I'm a little lucky so far today," said Mr. Fogg. "At least you haven't broken any glassware yet."

Henry couldn't think of anything to say. Just at that moment two women came to the counter and Mr. Fogg walked away.

The first woman said, "I need a wedding present

for my niece. I think a glass vase would make a nice present."

Henry lifted down several vases. The woman chose a small, graceful vase with a flower design.

"This is the only one in stock. I'm not allowed to sell this sample," Henry explained when he could not find another vase.

The woman looked unhappy, and Henry said, "I can order the vase for you and have it here in four days."

He took the order form from under the counter. "It's a beautiful vase," he said.

"Yes, it is," agreed the woman. "It's just what I want. You order it, and I'll be back early next week."

When the two women had gone, Henry filled out the order form for the vase. He filled in every blank and read the order over twice. He could find no errors. Doris approved the form and turned it over to Mr. Fogg.

Henry reported his first day of work to the family

that evening. "I hardly saw you at all, Ben," he said. "What was your day like?"

Benny smiled. "I didn't see Mr. Fogg for most of the day. But I did meet Miss Douglas."

"What did you think of her?" asked Violet.

"I don't know. She came down the stairs to the basement. She said that she was lost. But somehow I think that she wanted to look around. She said she was happy to meet me because I'll be delivering her purchases."

Benny stopped talking for a moment and looked puzzled.

"What's the matter?" asked Jessie.

"There was one strange thing about talking with Miss Douglas. She called me by my name, 'Benny Alden.' Now how did she know who I was? We had never met before. Maybe I'll find out tomorrow when I go to Woodland Path, that's where Miss Douglas lives."

"Some of the store people don't like her," said Henry. "One of them told me she's fussy and hard to please. Others won't wait on her if they can help it."

"That Miss Douglas is a mystery," said Jessie. "Who would think there'd be a mystery in a department store?"

CHAPTER 5

The Hidden House

It was Wednesday morning, and Benny was busy unpacking notebooks and writing paper. Mr. Fogg came over to him.

"I have a delivery for Miss Douglas. It's a special order, and she's in a hurry for it. You know where Woodland Path is, don't you? I don't want you to waste time."

Toni had given Benny directions. He started out

on his bike, sure that he would have no trouble. But it seemed that Woodland Path was almost impossible to find.

Benny reached the woods quickly, but finding the Path was a different matter.

"This looks like a path," Benny said out loud to himself. He took the box from his bike carrier. He left his bike out of sight, but close to the path. He started to push tree branches and blackberry vines away from his face.

Several times Benny thought he must be on the wrong path. How could a small woman like Miss Douglas come through such a tangle?

Just as he was thinking of turning back, he saw a house. It was not at all the kind of house he had expected to see. Could Miss Douglas live here?

Benny found that the path had taken him to the back door of the house. He followed a walk around to the front of the house. There he read the words "Woodland Path" carved on a small signboard hanging from a post. He saw a lane leading through the trees. The way he had come was probably a short-cut, Benny thought.

Benny went to the front door. He had to make his delivery and get back to the store. He knocked at the screen door. He could see inside because the front door itself was open. In fact, he couldn't help seeing inside.

What he saw amazed him. The living room was square, with a soft green carpet. Sun shining through a window lighted gold-and-white wall-paper. How could Miss Douglas dress so plainly when she lived in such a beautiful place?

Benny knocked again. He stepped back because he felt someone was watching him from behind a curtain. But no one came to the door.

"This is strange," thought Benny. Then he was surprised to see a boy come around the corner of the house.

"She isn't home," the boy said, as if he knew what Benny was thinking. "Nobody's home. You can leave the package by the door. It'll be safe. I'll tell

her you left it. You're from Furman's Department
Store, aren't you?"

"Yes, but how did you know?" asked Benny. He
felt taken by surprise, and he didn't like it.

"Easy," laughed the boy. "First, the box says
'Furman's' in big letters. And second, she's always
getting things delivered here. Only the deliveryman
usually comes down the lane."

"I've got to get back," Benny said, and looked at
his watch. "I'm working. Thank you for helping
me."

"It's OK," the boy said. "Don't worry about the
box." He sat down on the front step.

Benny walked around the house. When he was
out of the boy's sight, he ran down the path. As he
picked up his bicycle he wondered if Toni knew
what kind of house Miss Douglas had. And who was
the boy? Benny wished he knew.

By the time Benny got back to the store, it was
almost half past eleven.

"I thought we were going to close without you,"

said Toni. "The store is only open half a day on Wednesdays. That makes up for the evening hours we have."

Benny said, "I had forgotten all about that."

"Your sisters are here," Toni told him. "I think they're shopping until you and Henry can go. Mr. Fogg has something he wants you to do. You'd better see him right away."

Violet was on the second floor of the department store, looking at blouses. She was trying to find a blouse to wear with her new skirt.

She took a blouse off the rack and put it back. She was looking at a peach-colored one when she heard someone say, "No, no, my child, that style won't do! And the color is all wrong."

Violet turned around and faced a tiny woman. At first Violet wasn't sure the woman was talking to her. But there was no one else in sight.

A salesclerk came over to help Violet. "This one should fit you, and it's a good match for your skirt," she said.

"No, don't buy that blouse either," said the small woman, who stepped between Violet and the salesclerk. "Not that blouse," she repeated. "Look at those seams—that blouse won't last more than a few washings."

Violet didn't know what to say. She could now see that the blouse was not well made. But why should anyone stop her from buying a blouse? And to look at this woman, no one would think she knew anything about clothes.

"Well, Miss Douglas, what should I get?" Violet asked, for by now she was sure who this was.

Maggie Douglas did not seem surprised that Violet knew her name. She just began talking, "You had the right idea in the first place. Get a pale lavender blouse to go with the darker lavender skirt. I'm surprised that Furman's has been selling blouses that are so poor. I will have to talk to the manager about this."

Just as suddenly as the woman had appeared, she was gone.

Violet looked at the salesclerk and they both laughed. Jessie heard the whole story when she joined her sister a few minutes later.

Jessie laughed, too. "I can see that the boys were telling the truth about Maggie Douglas. Let's go downstairs and get the steam iron. It will be a surprise for Mrs. McGregor when she comes back from vacation."

Just as they reached the counter with the irons, Violet tugged Jessie's arm. "Look! There's Miss Douglas. She's the one talking to that man."

The conversation grew louder. Miss Douglas was saying, ". . . but I want the Perfect toaster that does two slices, not this model that does four."

"I'm sorry, it's this or nothing," said the man.

"You needn't be rude with me, Mr. Fogg! If you really wanted to make a sale, you'd show me the catalog. It has several kinds of two-slice toasters. But never mind. I'll see if you're in a better mood when I come to the store tomorrow."

Jessie was going to ask about the steam irons when Benny came up the stairs with a package. "This is for your department, Mr. Fogg," he said politely.

"No, Alden, you've made a mistake," said Mr. Fogg impatiently. "These are skillets, but they're not electric ones. I wouldn't have thought anyone with your family name would make a mistake like that. Take the box to the end of the next aisle. You'll see the right place."

Benny didn't say a word, but his cheeks were red.

The two sisters looked at each other.

A buzzer made a loud sound. The girls heard a nearby clerk say, "Ten minutes until closing time."

"Let's buy this iron," said Violet, pointing to one on the counter.

"I'm not sure," Jessie answered. "We'll have to talk to Mr. Fogg." She quickly ran to where Mr. Fogg was standing. She did not let his cross look stop her from asking, "Can you help us choose an iron?"

"No, young lady. It's closing time. I have to close out my sales book, and you should be leaving the store." And with that, Mr. Fogg walked away.

Jessie turned around helplessly and started to walk back toward Violet. Mr. Furman came up to her and asked, "Do you need some help?"

"I guess it is pretty late to be shopping, but I do want to get a new steam iron today," Jessie explained.

"That's no problem," said Mr. Furman. "Here's your brother Henry. I'll send him down for a new iron that just came this morning. You'd do me a favor to test it."

Benny was waiting near the front of the store.

Mr. Furman laughed. "It takes the whole Alden family to make a purchase."

Jessie paid for the steam iron and the Aldens were on their way home.

"I must say your Mr. Fogg is difficult," said Jessie. "But I can see that Miss Douglas is even more of a character. Things can't be dull at the store."

"That's for sure," said Benny. "I like the work. I never know what will happen next. Most of the people have been pleasant, even when I make mistakes. They know I haven't worked at the store very long and it's easy to forget things. But you know, I never knew there were any problems in a department store. I thought the manager just ordered things and the customers came in to buy them."

Jessie nodded. "I guess you have to work at a job before you know how much there is to it."

"You can see Mr. Fogg is always grumpy," Benny added. "I'm not going to let him get me down, though. That might ruin my appetite, and it's lunchtime."

The other Aldens laughed. They knew that it would take much more than Mr. Fogg to stop Benny from being hungry.

While he ate lunch, Benny thought about Miss Douglas and her house in the woods and about the boy he had met. Were these all pieces in a puzzle? Benny couldn't make up his mind. He decided to keep his eyes and ears open, but nothing happened during the rest of the week—nothing except that Benny and Henry got their first pay envelopes.

"Now this makes it a real job," Benny said with a smile.

CHAPTER 6

Who Wrote the Letters?

Monday morning was almost gone before Henry remembered the order for the glass vase. He checked with Mrs. Lester.

"No, Henry, I haven't seen any package," Doris said. "You might ask the other clerks. Sometimes a package is taken to the wrong department."

Henry checked with almost everyone in the store. No one had seen his order. There was no extra package of any kind to be found.

Doris could see that Henry was worried. "I think I'll call the company and see if the order has been sent out," she told him.

"Thank you, Doris. I'm certain the customer will be in. I promised she would have the vase today."

Benny came by. "I'm going to get the mail for the departments," he said. By now, handing out the mail was one of his regular jobs.

"See if you can find a glass vase for me," Henry said.

Benny laughed and answered, "I'll try." But of course Mr. Furman gave Benny only letters, catalogs, and advertisements to deliver throughout the store.

Usually Benny did not stop to look through the mail before he began to give it out. But this time he glanced through the letters as he left Mr. Furman's office.

Benny stared. To his surprise there was a letter addressed, "Benny Alden, care of Furman's Department Store."

Benny turned the envelope this way and that. It was an ordinary post office envelope with a printed stamp. Benny carefully tore open his letter. He found a sheet of blue writing paper. The written message was short. It said, "Your work for Furman's Store has been excellent. It is noticed and it is appreciated."

"What in the world?" thought Benny.

He was pleased, but he was more puzzled than pleased. Who could have sent him this? He thought to himself, "It must be somebody who is in the store, because who else would know? Mr. Furman? Toni? Doris? This is a mystery!"

He thought of showing the letter to Toni, but suppose she had written it? She might think Benny wasn't very smart to ask her. So Benny carefully put the letter in his pocket. He passed out the mail as if nothing had happened.

He had just given a thick envelope to Mr. Fogg when someone said, "Hi, Benny! Remember me?"

Benny turned around quickly. "Sure," he said.

"You were at Woodland Path when I took the package there."

"That's right," said the boy. "I told the lady you brought it. You came through the woods, so I guess you rode your bike away."

Benny was going to say, "You're a good detective. How do you know my name?" when Mr. Fogg spoke.

"That's enough standing around, Alden. Go down and help the man in the basement. See if he has those bowls for the electric mixers. I need them."

"Yes, sir," Benny said and hurried off. Some people said Mr. Fogg was hard to get along with because he had a painful back. If that was so, it still did not make Benny like to be bossed around.

Benny thought about the boy whose name he didn't know. And yet the boy knew Benny's name. That was another puzzle. He felt as if the boy was teasing him. But there was no time to think about that.

Benny was so busy the rest of the day that he did not think about anything but work. He forgot about his mystery letter until dinnertime. Then he showed it to his grandfather.

"Well, Benny," said Mr. Alden, "this is very good. I like to have my grandchildren appreciated. Who sent it?"

"I haven't any idea," Benny replied. "No one signed it. I never saw writing like this before. But anyone could buy the envelope."

Jessie said, "Let me see." She took the letter and read it. "It's nice writing and it looks strong, somehow. It could be either a man's writing or a woman's. I can't tell."

Violet looked at the letter, too. She laughed and said, "Now you have a small mystery, Benny. You should like that."

"I have a mystery, too," Henry said. "But not like Benny's. I ordered a vase for a customer. It should have come by now, but it hasn't." Henry told the Aldens about the order.

"What did Mrs. Lester tell you about her phone call?" asked Jessie.

"She told me that the order had been sent."

"How could the box get lost?" Violet asked.

"I asked Doris the same thing," said Henry. "She said that it wasn't hard. The store once lost a bass drum." Everyone laughed.

"Did she order another vase?" asked Jessie.

"Yes, she did. It should get here in time for my customer. But I had to call the woman so that she wouldn't make a trip to the store for nothing."

"That was a thoughtful thing to do," said Mr. Alden.

"Was it Miss Douglas who ordered the vase?" asked Violet.

"No, the woman's name was Mrs. Allen," Henry said. "She seemed satisfied that Furman's was doing the best it could."

"But you're not satisfied, are you, Henry?" asked Grandfather. "What's the matter?"

Henry took a long breath and said, "Grandfather,

you don't suppose that Mr. Fogg has anything to do with this? He seems to want to make trouble for Ben and me. He keeps saying that Aldens shouldn't make mistakes."

"Don't worry, Henry," Mr. Alden said. "I'm sure the vase will turn up, and I doubt that Mr. Fogg has anything to do with it."

The next day when Benny handed out the mail, he gave a letter to Doris. The envelope was exactly like the one Benny had received.

Doris said what Benny thought she would. "Who can be writing to me in care of the store? Why wasn't the letter sent to my house?"

"You'll never know unless you open it," Benny said, and he tried to sound mysterious.

Doris tore open her letter and took out a sheet of blue writing paper. She blushed.

Benny couldn't help asking, "What's the matter?"

"I can't read this out loud. You read it," she said. "Is this a joke or something?"

Benny read aloud, "You are the kind of salesperson who always keeps your customer's likes and dislikes in mind. Good."

"This is true," said Benny. "But I wonder who is watching us. See—I got a letter, too." And he pulled the blue notepaper out of his pocket.

This was beginning to be exciting, at least to Benny and Doris. They weren't surprised when the next mail brought a letter for Toni. It read, "You are a fine cashier. You're never too busy to say 'Thank you' as you count out the change."

Henry received a letter, too. It said, "Do not feel upset about your work. You are thoughtful about your customers."

"Now this is too much!" exclaimed Benny. "Who would know something has been bothering you? We'll have to do some detective work and find out who is sending these notes."

"I know one person who didn't write this," Henry said grimly. "Mr. Fogg!"

Some of the other workers also had notes. One person teased Benny by saying, "Are you doing

this, Benny Alden? Nothing like this ever happened
before you came to work."

Benny shook his head. "There was a letter for me,
too," he said. "I'm going to keep it in my locker.
Then it will be handy to read after Mr. Fogg scolds
me."

"Well," laughed the salesclerk, "you're a smart
boy. Maybe you wrote one to yourself just to fool
everyone."

"I want to be smart enough to find out who really
sent these notes," Benny answered.

"Let me know when you find out," said the clerk.
"I think it's a big joke of some kind."

But it was no joke when a note came for Mr.
Fogg. Benny didn't want to give the letter to him.
He handed the envelope to Henry. Henry handed it
to Toni. Toni handed the envelope to Doris.

"All right," Mrs. Lester said. "I'll take this to Mr.
Fogg. But I wonder what nice thing the mystery
writer can say about Mr. Fogg."

Mr. Fogg grunted as he took the envelope from

Doris. He opened it and frowned. He did not show the letter to anyone. He just crushed it in his hand and threw it toward the wastebasket. His toss missed. The crumpled ball of paper fell at Mrs. Lester's feet.

"It's nothing," Mr. Fogg said, trying to sound as though he didn't care about the letter. "Someone around here is playing practical jokes." He glared at Benny, who was standing near Henry's counter.

"And if I catch whoever is sending these crazy letters, there'll be trouble." Mr. Fogg turned around to arrange the stock on his shelves.

Doris went to a corner out of Mr. Fogg's sight. "He threw this away," she told Benny and held up the letter Mr. Fogg had tossed away. "I just have to see what it says."

She smoothed out the crumpled paper. "It says, 'You hurt business. Furman's needs more polite behavior from its first floor manager.'"

"There," said Benny. "Justice at last."

"But who writes these notes?" asked Mrs. Lester. "Who knows everyone so well?"

"I'm going to find out," promised Benny. "Mr. Fogg wants to blame Henry and me. I'll prove he's wrong."

The managers of some of the other departments began to walk past Benny and Doris. "Are you coming to Mr. Furman's office?" someone asked her.

"Oh, I forgot about the meeting Mr. Furman called," Doris said. "Henry is supposed to come, too. I'd better remind him. I'll see you later, Benny."

Henry felt out of place at the meeting, especially when Mr. Fogg said pointedly, "I don't think a boy belongs here."

Mr. Furman said, "I asked Mrs. Lester to bring Henry. I feel he is interested in the store. This is a good chance for him to see how we do business."

Henry listened as the department managers talked. At last Mr. Furman turned to Henry and said, "Do you have anything to report? Is everything all right?"

Henry blurted out, "I'm sorry about the double order for the expensive glass vase. I don't know what happened. I've looked all over the store for the first one. It was supposed to be here, but no one has seen it."

That was all Mr. Fogg needed. "See!" he exclaimed. "I told you that these Aldens are more trouble than they are worth."

Mr. Furman surprised everyone by laughing. "I

have two things to say. First, I have a story to tell
you. This morning a woman came up the stairs to
my office and knocked on my door. I asked her if she
had a complaint to make. 'No,' she said. 'I have a
compliment to give.'"

Everyone at the meeting was listening to Mr.
Furman. He continued, "Hardly anyone takes the
time to praise our salespeople, so I was interested in
what she had to say. She was helped by our new
glassware clerk, Henry, and by our delivery boy,
Benny. And Henry, here's the second thing I have
to say. I can make you feel better about that vase in a
few minutes. Follow me."

The meeting was over and Mr. Furman led the
way down the stairs and to the glassware department. Henry and the others followed. Out of the
corner of his eye, Henry saw Miss Douglas, but she
was busy with one of the clerks.

"I'll explain the mystery of the missing vase," Mr.
Furman said. "The other day I looked over the mail
before Benny took it to the different departments.

There was a special delivery package with a label that said 'Glassware.' I knew it had to go to Mrs. Lester, so I thought I'd deliver it myself. And I did, right to this spot."

Henry, Doris, Mr. Fogg, the department heads—all trooped over to the place where Mr. Furman was standing.

On the floor under the counter, almost out of sight, was the missing package.

Even Mr. Fogg admitted, "I've been by here several times and I never saw that package. It's in the shadows there. Anyone could miss it."

"We all did," said Henry. He picked up the box and began to unwrap it. "I'll make a special display and try to sell this before the day is over."

Henry then smiled at Mr. Furman and the people around him.

He even smiled at Mr. Fogg. But Mr. Fogg looked as cross as ever. And when Mr. Fogg saw Miss Douglas walking in his direction, his frown became a real scowl.

CHAPTER 7

A New Puzzle

One mystery was solved. Mr. Fogg had not had anything to do with the missing vase. But soon there was another mystery.

Benny came early the next morning, but Toni and Doris were already in the store. Sam, the night watchman, had let them in before he went home.

"Help me fold these dust covers, Benny," Doris

called. "I have to set up the jewelry display. We're advertising our jewelry in the paper today. A lot of people should come in. It will be a busy day."

Benny helped lift and fold the blue cloths used to cover the glass counters at night.

Doris began to set out boxes with rings and pins. Suddenly she said, "What's this?"

She picked up a box she had found under the counter. It held lockets and silver chains. Each locket was filled with a pleasant flower perfume.

"Where did these come from?" she asked. "Toni, did you order them? I must have a dozen of these lockets."

Toni walked over to look at the lockets. She shook her head. "No, I didn't order these. But I saw some advertised in a New York paper. Do you think they'll sell in Greenfield?"

Doris said, "Perhaps Mr. Furman ordered them. The price tags are on the lockets. I'll ask him as soon as I see him."

But when Doris saw Mr. Furman he said, "No, I

didn't order them. I have no idea how they got here. Did you ask Mr. Fogg?"

Mr. Fogg only shook a finger at Doris and said gruffly, "How would I know where those lockets came from? I'm just the first floor manager, that's all. Who pays attention to me?"

"I've heard of shoplifting," Toni told Doris. "But I have never heard of new merchandise just mysteriously appearing."

Benny heard Toni say this because he had come to get an order from her to deliver. He asked, "Do you suppose someone came in the store after it was closed yesterday?"

Toni shook her head. "The watchman must have been here and the man who cleans after the store is closed. Mr. Furman and Mr. Fogg have keys. I suppose the new owner has one, too, but he's in New York. I don't think anyone else has a key."

"If it wasn't Mr. Furman or Mr. Fogg, who could it be?" asked Benny. But there was no answer.

Miss Douglas had come in, and everyone was

watching her. She walked quickly toward the jewelry counter.

"I wonder if she'll buy one of the mystery lockets," Toni said to Benny.

But Miss Douglas asked Doris to show her the earrings. Some of the salespeople smiled at the idea of plain Maggie Douglas wearing earrings.

In a few minutes Miss Douglas went toward Mr. Fogg's department. He turned away as if he hoped she would pass him by.

"Now what?" wondered Toni aloud to Benny. "You'd think she'd have a shopping list with her. She wouldn't have to make so many trips."

"I guess," Benny said slowly, "that Maggie Douglas wants to be at Furman's every day. I think she must be lonesome."

"Benny, you're quite a boy to think of that," said Toni. "You may be right. Here, be sure to deliver this box right away. I promised an early delivery on it."

Mr. Fogg called to Benny, "There is another

order to deliver, too. I expect to see you back before lunchtime. Don't just stand around talking."

"See here, Mr. Fogg," Maggie Douglas interrupted. "I want to look at coffeemakers today. What kinds do you have?"

No one else ever spoke to Mr. Fogg in such a sharp voice. Miss Douglas never let Mr. Fogg's rudeness stop her.

Benny couldn't wait to see what happened next. He had his deliveries to make. But he could guess that Mr. Fogg would pay as little attention as possible to Miss Douglas. He always expected trouble from her visits.

In the basement stockroom Benny picked up another delivery. It was one Miss Douglas had ordered. By now Benny knew the way to Woodland Path very well. If he hurried, he could make his morning deliveries and be back before noon.

At his first stop, Benny did not have to knock. "Well, I should think it was about time," said a sharp voice from inside a screen door. "Furman's

Department Store always says it will deliver orders promptly."

A woman with a pointed nose and a small mouth turned down at the corners faced Benny.

Benny smiled as pleasantly as he could. "We were glad to have your order. I hope it's right," he said as he gave her a small box.

"Well," replied the woman, "why don't you go back to the store? Are you nosey? Do you want to know what is in this box?"

Benny answered, "I thought I'd see if your order is right. If it isn't, I can take it back now and save another trip."

"Always thinking of yourself—save yourself some work," the woman said. "You say that you deliver free any purchase within the city limits."

"Yes, we do," said Benny. He did not say that this house was just a short distance beyond the city limits. He thought the woman knew it very well.

The woman took the package and unwrapped it. She opened a little white box. There lay a beautiful pin made with pearls.

"I guess my granddaughter will like that," she said. "It's for her eighteenth birthday. She'll have so many gifts she won't even notice it."

"Would you like to have me take it back to the store and put birthday paper and ribbon on it?" Benny asked. "We could put it in a stronger box and mail it for you." He thought there had to be some way to please this customer.

"Well, now," said the woman. "I never thought of that. Take the gift back and do just that." At last she smiled. "I will say you are a good delivery boy."

Benny took the box and said, "Please give me the name you want written on the gift card."

The woman disappeared for a moment. She came back with the name. "Fill out the card just as I have it," she said. "Send me a bill for whatever extra charge there may be."

As Benny rode to make his next delivery he thought to himself, "People are so different. That customer was cross for no reason. It's hard not to be cross right back. But I didn't want to lose a customer for Furman's."

The next delivery was no trouble. Then Benny was on his way down the path through the woods to Miss Douglas's house. He knew from the box that Miss Douglas had ordered a bird feeder.

As Benny got ready to knock on the door he saw the boy he'd met before at Woodland Path.

"I thought you'd be along soon," the boy said. "The bird feeder isn't for Miss Maggie. It's for her neighbor. Here's the name and address, see?" He gave Benny a slip of blue paper with a name and address written on it.

Benny put the paper in his pocket, picked up the box with the bird feeder in it, and followed the boy. They soon came to a house almost hidden by trees.

"Here we are, Mrs. Fields," the boy called. "Benny from the department store has the new bird feeder."

When Mrs. Fields came to the door Benny asked in a surprised voice, "How are you going to set this up? The picture on the box shows the bird feeder hung from ropes between the house and a tree."

"I really don't know," said Mrs. Fields. "I love the wild birds here. A cat just broke my old feeder and scared the birds away. As you can see, I've had a bad sprain. That's why my ankle is bandaged. I suppose the directions with the feeder will tell what to do with it."

"They do," said Benny. "But you need a ladder to put it up properly. The bird feeder has to hang from a rope between your window and a tree. You can pull the feeder to your window to fill it and then slide it out on the rope."

Benny was so busy talking to Mrs. Fields that he did not notice that the boy was gone. Now he came from the garage, carrying a ladder.

"Come on, Ben," the boy called. "Let's put up the feeder for Mrs. Fields."

"What kind boys you are," exclaimed Mrs. Fields. "And how nice my neighbor asked you to put the feeder up for me. I wanted to see the birds because I can't move around very much until my ankle is better."

The boys almost had the feeder in place. But Mrs. Fields could not wait. She threw a handful of

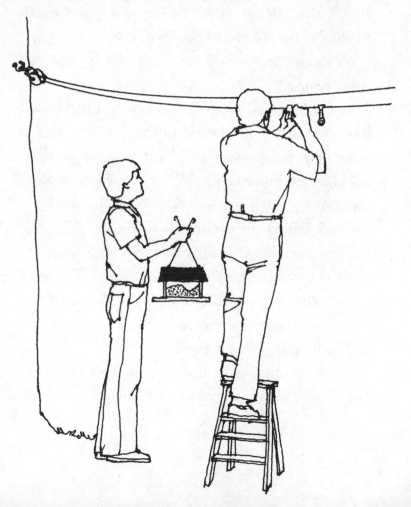

sunflower seeds into the driveway. Suddenly there was a flutter of wings, and the boys saw chickadees, blue jays, woodpeckers, and juncos.

"I guess they're pretty happy to have a new feeder, too," Benny said. "I'd like to stay and watch the birds. But I have to get back to work."

As Benny started off, the boy called, "See you later, Benny."

Benny felt good about the deliveries he had made. But after lunch Mr. Fogg called, "Alden, this is something for you to do. That Maggie Douglas called a few minutes ago. Why she wants another coffeemaker is beyond me. Go downstairs and see if we have a Brewrite coffeemaker in stock."

"Yes, Mr. Fogg," Benny said quickly.

"If you have one, just take it out to the woman. I don't want to be bothered with this anymore this afternoon." Then he put his hand on his back and said to himself, "What a pain!"

A few minutes later Benny went upstairs to see Mr. Fogg. "What is it now?" Mr. Fogg asked. "My back aches, and you make my head ache."

"Well, Mr. Fogg," Benny began. "We don't have the Brewrite coffeemaker. The only one we have is the Peerless. At least that's the one Miss Douglas doesn't have yet." Benny couldn't help smiling because it did seem odd that she had at least four other coffeemakers already.

"This may be a funny matter to you, but it isn't to me," Mr. Fogg almost shouted. "My time is more important than that Miss Douglas seems to think it is. Even your time is more important, Alden. Box up one of the Peerless models and take it out to her. With any luck at all, she won't notice the difference. Or if she does, it won't be worth complaining about."

"Don't you think you should call and ask if she wants this one?" asked Benny.

"Just do as I say, Alden," said Mr. Fogg. "I'm the manager, remember."

"Yes, sir," Benny answered and went downstairs. He found the coffeemaker and was soon headed for the revolving door at the front of the store.

Carrying the box, Benny tried to push the door. Someone else was pushing it, too. Benny heard a laugh, and he knew who it was. The boy who lived near Miss Douglas was laughing at him.

Benny stepped back. The other boy stepped back. Now Benny began to laugh, too.

Toni, who was watching, called, "You two look as if you are dancing." She began to laugh.

By now the boys were caught in the door. Mr. Furman came by. He pushed the door just a little and Benny squeezed out. Soon the other boy stood beside him.

When Benny could stop laughing, he asked, "Did Miss Douglas want you to get this coffeemaker?"

The boy shook his head. "No, she asked me to give her that slip with Mrs. Fields' name and address on it. You know, that's the lady who has the new bird feeder. I don't know why Miss Maggie wants that slip. Maybe it has something else written on it. I told her I had given it to you."

Benny put down the box he was carrying. He felt in his pockets. It seemed unusual that Miss Douglas needed the slip of paper. But a lot of things were unusual about Miss Douglas, Benny thought.

He pulled out several papers he had folded together. He found the blue slip of paper. He unfolded it. As he looked at the writing he felt sure he had seen that kind of writing before. Where?

"That's it!" the boy said. "Give it to me and I'll return it. I have another errand to do."

Benny put the box with the coffeemaker into the carrier on his bike. Why was the scrap of paper important? He had not seen anything except Mrs. Fields' name and address on it. He could not think of a reason, so he soon forgot the whole thing. Mr. Fogg would really complain if he did not hurry.

As he rode along, Benny remembered the mystery of the silver lockets. He'd have to ask Henry if anyone had solved that. Things were going on at Furman's Department Store that Benny just couldn't understand.

CHAPTER 8

Henry's Adventure

On their way to work the next morning Benny and Henry talked about the mystery of the lockets.

Henry said, "No one could find out how the lockets got to the jewelry counter. At first it seemed as if someone was playing a joke."

"I know," said Benny. "It did seem funny."

"The more Mr. Furman thought about it, the more it worried him," Henry went on. "He called in a locksmith and had the front door lock changed yesterday afternoon. He has a new key, and he gave one to Mr. Fogg. He mailed one to the new owner in New York."

The boys had just reported for work when Mr. Furman called Henry to his office.

"I have no one else I can ask," he began. "I have a real problem. The man who comes to work at six o'clock is sick and won't be here. Sam does not start to work until midnight. I need someone to sweep the floor and empty the wastebaskets. I don't have anyone to do the work."

Henry smiled. "If you think I can do the work, I'll try. Just tell me what has to be done."

"That's fine, Henry. I hoped you would say that," exclaimed Mr. Furman. "Some people won't do that kind of work after they've been salespeople."

As Mr. Furman finished speaking, there was a knock on the office door. "Come in," he called.

Sam, the nightwatchman, stood in the doorway. "You wanted to talk to me?" he asked.

"Yes, Sam. Did everything go all right last night?"

"All quiet," Sam said. "Not a bit of trouble."

"Good," said Mr. Furman. "Sam, tell me again about what happened the night before. We're still trying to find out how those lockets got on the jewelry counter."

"Don't you mind staying alone all night?" Henry asked.

"No," Sam said. "I'm used to it. Here's what happened the other night," he continued, turning to Mr. Furman. "I was making my rounds on the first floor, the way I always do. It was about one o'clock in the morning. I thought I heard a sound, like footsteps."

"Yes?" said Mr. Furman. "Go on."

"I listened. Everything was quiet. I flashed my light around to see if anything was going on."

"And you didn't see anything at all?"

"Well, no. Somebody must have been decorating the store windows. There was a dress dummy near the window by the front door. I hadn't noticed it when I came in. But I could have missed seeing it then."

Mr. Furman wrote a note on a pad on his desk. "Please go on," he said to Sam.

"So everything seemed OK. I went down to the basement to check. I wasn't down there long. I was coming up the stairs when I said to myself, 'There's got to be something wrong.' I just had that feeling—something was wrong. Then I heard it. The front door clicked shut. It was soft, but I heard it. I ran over and looked out. 'Stop!' I yelled."

"You saw something outside?" Henry asked.

"Naw. Not a soul. I looked both ways. Nothing."

"Do you think perhaps you just thought you heard the door close?" Mr. Furman asked.

"I heard it. I'm sure of it," Sam said. "I don't make things up."

"All right," said Mr. Furman. "So that's a clue we can work on. Did you look around the first floor again?"

"Sure. Everything was OK." Suddenly Sam stopped. "Wait a minute! Something kind of bothered me, though. Now I know what it was. You know that dress dummy I saw by the front window? I don't think I saw it again. It was gone. Come to think of it now, I'm sure it was missing. Now what do you think of that?"

"I don't know what to think," Mr. Furman said. "But we had the lock on the door changed yesterday afternoon. Did you see or hear anything before the store opened this morning?"

"Like I said before, everything was quiet last night," Sam said, getting up to leave.

After the watchman had gone, Mr. Furman told Henry, "We did not want to alarm people yesterday. Someone was in the store. We're sure of that. Toni checked out her cash register and I looked around quietly to see if anyone had been in my office."

"Was anything missing?" Henry asked.

"Not that I could see. I asked Mr. Fogg to check

on the cameras and radios. Those are sometimes stolen. Nothing had been taken. And everything was all right on the second floor."

Henry could see that Mr. Furman was not satisfied. "I'll keep my eyes and ears open while I work this evening," he promised. "You can count on me."

Mr. Furman smiled at that. "Yes, I am sure I can. Go home now and report back when the store is closing. I'll just say you are absent today."

Henry wondered about that, and Mr. Furman explained, "I have one idea. Somebody could hide in the store at the end of the day. When the store is empty, the person could come out and do what he wanted to do. Some big stores keep watch dogs to sniff around and catch people doing that."

"Do you think it could be one of the store workers?" Henry asked. "It had to be somebody who knew the store well to put those price tags on the lockets."

Mr. Furman shrugged his shoulders. "I know. It's a puzzle."

"How could anyone get out if the doors were locked?" Henry said. "Someone who hid in the store after working hours wouldn't want to stay all night."

"That part is no problem," Mr. Furman said. "The doors can always be opened from the inside. It's a fire safety rule. But you have to have a key to get in from the outside. Unless someone lets you in. But I trust Sam. He would not do that."

Henry stood up. "I'll come back ready to go to work. Will I see you before I begin?"

"Yes, report to me. I may have some special instructions for you."

Henry went down to the basement stockroom and found Benny there. He told Benny about his special job. Then Henry went home, leaving by a back door.

Benny had a busy day. But for once he did not have a delivery to make for Miss Douglas. In fact, Miss Douglas did not come into the store at all that day. By the end of the afternoon the salespeople were wondering what had happened to her.

Benny was ready to leave when he saw Henry talking to Mr. Furman. He was wearing work clothes. Mr. Furman was showing him where the floor brushes and big trash bins were.

"Don't worry about the second floor," he told Henry. "I want you to spend your time on the first floor. You can turn on the lights while you're sweeping. Check all the offices, washrooms, and the basement to be sure the building is empty. That's important. If you see anything suspicious, phone me right away."

"Not the police?" asked Henry.

"I don't think we need the police," Mr. Furman said. "No one has done anything wrong. That is what is so puzzling about this."

The store was soon quiet. Henry checked the doors to be sure they were locked. He went up to the second floor to make sure it was empty. He switched on the lights. The dust covers on the counters made the store look different and spooky. He went back to the room where dresses and coats hung on long racks. He stooped down to make sure no one was there. Everything was all right.

Next, Henry went to the basement stockroom. Up and down the aisles of boxes he went. He stopped to listen. There was not a sound. He picked up the long floor brush and started upstairs.

He opened the door and stood still. Did he hear someone walking softly around? Something fell and Henry jumped.

Carefully, quietly, step by step, Henry slipped through the door and stood in the shadow by the water fountain.

Someone tall was walking around with a limping step, back bent, lifting the dust covers on the counters and putting them back.

Henry had to decide what to do. Should he call out "Stop!" or go down to the basement and telephone Mr. Furman? Perhaps Mr. Furman would not be at home yet. The store had not been closed long.

Henry took a step forward. Just at that moment

the figure whirled around and faced him. Henry
gasped.

It was Mr. Fogg!

For a second neither Henry nor Mr. Fogg spoke.
Then Mr. Fogg exclaimed, "I knew it was you! But

nobody would listen to me. Now I can prove it!"

"Me!" Henry said. "What do you mean? I'm doing my job, that's all. What are you doing here? I thought everyone had gone home."

"You thought!" said Mr. Fogg angrily. "You're so nice, so hard working, so polite! I know what you are doing. Trying to get me into trouble, that's all. Well, you can't."

By now Henry was angry, too. But he knew that he could not get anywhere by fighting Mr. Fogg.

"Wait," Henry said. "How can I get you in trouble? You're the first floor manager. Mr. Furman trusts you and depends on you."

"I know what you did," Mr. Fogg exclaimed. "Sneaking around and putting those lockets out. That was your work. Oh, yes, it was. I wouldn't be surprised if those lockets weren't made by some company your grandfather owns. Aldens want to run everything."

Henry shook his head. What could he say? He was beginning to believe it was Mr. Fogg who had put the lockets on the jewelry counter—for the very purpose of getting *Henry* in trouble.

As quietly as he could, Henry said, "I think there's some mistake. I never saw those lockets until Doris found them. Someone else put them there. It wasn't my work. I thought maybe you put them there."

"Me?" shouted Mr. Fogg. "Don't be stupid."

"Then why are you here after the store is closed?" asked Henry. "You have a key."

"I'm here to catch someone like you sneaking around, that's what."

Talking with Mr. Fogg was getting Henry nowhere. "Shall I phone Mr. Furman and ask him to come back?" he asked. "We can settle this right away."

Mr. Fogg shook his head. "Don't try to fool me that way. I'm ready to leave. I'll talk to Mr. Furman in the morning. If anything happens in the store tonight, then he will know who is to blame. Good night."

Henry watched as the man strode with a limp to the door and let it slam loudly behind him.

Pushing the big brush over the floor and emptying the wastebaskets gave Henry time to think. Now that he had cooled off, he decided that Mr. Fogg probably had nothing to do with the lockets. It was too wild an idea to suppose he could get the Aldens in trouble that way. So, how had the lockets gotten into the store?

Henry finished sweeping. He looked around. Everything was in place. He turned off the lights, but kept his flashlight handy. Then he had an idea.

Henry ran upstairs. Mr. Furman had told him not to sweep the second floor.

He now switched on all the lights upstairs as if he was going to work there.

If anyone was watching the store from the outside, that person would think the first floor was empty.

Then Henry went back to the first floor, moving carefully and quietly in the darkness. He held his flashlight ready. Near the front door he sat down and waited.

Time passed. The store was very quiet. Outside on the sidewalk a few people stopped to look at the store windows. Cars went by in the warm summer night.

Henry looked at his watch. What a long evening! He felt like giving up, but he didn't. Someone might still try to open the front door.

At last it was eleven o'clock. By now there was almost no traffic and no one walked by. Henry wondered how Sam could spend night after night as watchman. It wasn't the kind of work Henry would like to do all the time.

Henry was about to yawn when he heard something. Somebody was trying to push a key in the lock. Henry could hear it scrape. But the lock did not open. The door stayed closed.

After three times, whoever it was gave up. Henry counted to ten and then moved cautiously to the door. He looked out through the glass. Away down the street he saw a short figure getting into a car. He could not make out the license number. The car was soon driven off.

There was nothing Henry could do. In the morning he could tell Mr. Furman about what he had heard. He was sure of one thing. The figure had not belonged to Mr. Fogg. And anyway, Mr. Fogg had a new key and could have opened the door with no trouble.

When Sam came, Henry was glad to say good night. At home he found Benny still awake.

"Well?" asked Benny. "What happened?"

When he had heard Henry's story Benny said, "It's a real mystery. Yes, sir, a real mystery. And we'll find the answers. You'll see."

CHAPTER 9

Benny Has Ideas

Benny saw Henry and Mr. Fogg go into Mr. Furman's office. He half expected to hear shouting and angry voices. There was nothing of the kind. Soon Mr. Fogg and Henry walked out together. Neither one looked angry or even upset. Benny couldn't imagine what had gone on in Mr. Furman's office.

Mr. Fogg called, "Here, Alden. Take this Brew-rite coffeemaker to Miss Douglas. It seems you were right. She already has the Peerless."

Benny could hardly believe his ears. Was Mr. Fogg for once saying that Benny was right? What had happened to make Mr. Fogg behave so differently? Maybe his back was better!

With the box holding the coffeemaker set safely in his bicycle carrier, Benny rode off to Woodland Path. He knocked at the door and had a new surprise. Miss Douglas herself answered and asked him to come in.

"Benny Alden," she said, "you've been here many times, but we have always missed each other."

"Yes, ma'am," Benny said. He felt mixed-up. First Mr. Fogg had not acted as Benny had expected. And now Miss Douglas, too, seemed like a new and different person.

"This is a warm morning," she said. "Would you like some fruit juice and cookies before you ride back? Bring the coffeemaker and we'll go into the kitchen."

Benny stepped into a sunny kitchen with plants hanging in the windows. To see Miss Douglas in

Furman's Department Store, anyone would expect
her kitchen to be dark and old-fashioned. Instead,
everything was new and bright.

Benny put the coffeemaker down on the counter.
There were four other coffeemakers already there.

Miss Douglas knew that Benny was curious.
"Why do I need five different coffeemakers? I'll tell
you. I have a hobby. I like to test new products. I
keep a score for each item, then I know which is
best." She pointed to a sheet of paper, filled with
strong, clear writing. "So far, the Peerless is the best
of these coffeemakers. But the Brewrite could be
better."

Going to the refrigerator, she poured juice for
Benny and offered him cookies.

"I really can't stay," Benny said. "Mr. Fogg
doesn't like to have me stop when I'm making
deliveries."

"Mr. Fogg!" laughed Miss Douglas. "He tries to
act like an old bear. Sometimes he really makes you
think that's what he is."

"Well, yes . . ." Benny said, not knowing just how to understand what Miss Douglas had said.

"I hear someone knocking," she said. "Excuse me while I see who it is."

Benny heard her exclaim, "Come in, Ted! Benny is here now. He's having something cool to drink. It's such a hot morning already."

Miss Douglas led a boy Benny's size into the kitchen. "Hi!" the boy said, like an old friend.

"Do you two know each other?" asked Miss Douglas. "Benny Alden, this is my neighbor and good errand boy, Ted Evans. What have you there, Ted? Did you get the box from the post office?"

"Here's the box and some letters, too," Ted said.

Benny could not see the address on the box, but the wrapping paper had the words "Newport Fine Jewelry" made into a design. And Benny noticed that the word "Forward" was written on a letter that looked as if it was from Furman's Department Store.

"Do you have many deliveries today?" Ted asked

Benny. "It's too warm to do anything."

"Just this one for Miss Douglas," Benny answered. "I think I'll work in the stockroom in the basement. Anyway, it's cool in the store."

"Well," Ted said, "I'm going swimming at the park pool. Too bad you can't come."

The kitchen clock's ticking reminded Benny that time was passing. He got up quickly and thanked Miss Douglas for the chance to rest.

"I'll see you here again," Miss Douglas said. "I understand you will be back in school soon. August is almost over."

"I wish it weren't," Benny said. "I like to work in the store. But how did you know I just have a summer job?"

"Oh, I learn a little here and something else there," Miss Douglas said. "It's surprising how much you can learn if no one thinks you are paying attention."

As Benny rode back to Furman's, he thought about what Miss Douglas had said. He began to put

some ideas together. At last he said, "It can't be
true. I have to be wrong."

Back at the store, Benny reported to Mr. Fogg.
He took the Peerless coffeemaker without saying
anything. Then Benny went down to the basement,
where he had a locker. It was such a hot morning
that he had not worn even a sweater, so his locker
was empty. Except for one thing. He had put the
mystery letter, the one he had received when he
began working, on the locker shelf.

Benny took the letter down and opened it. He
looked thoughtfully at the writing and the blue
paper. "I wish I could really compare this," he said
to himself. "I think I'm right, but I can't be sure."

Later in the morning, Doris needed more cups
and saucers for her department. Benny carried them
up to her.

"Are all those lockets sold?" he asked.

"Yes, every one. I'm ordering a dozen more."

"Who makes them?" Benny asked. "Did you find
them listed in a catalog?"

Doris laughed. "I suppose I could have. But the name of the maker was on the box. That's how I found out where to order them."

"Do you remember the name?"

"Oh, Newberry or Newport or Portland. I can't remember right now. If you really want to know I can look it up." '

"It's all right," Benny said. "I was just curious."

At lunchtime Benny and Henry took their sandwiches and ate them in the park. Benny looked around to make sure no one was near.

Then Benny said, "I have an idea about Maggie Douglas, but no one will believe it. I don't think she's Maggie Douglas at all."

Henry didn't say a word. He took a big bite out of his ham-and-cheese sandwich. Then he looked at his brother and winked slowly.

"What does that mean?" asked Benny.

"It means I think you are getting close to the mysteries we have had at the store."

"What makes you think so?"

"I don't know too much," Henry said. "I just know a little piece. This morning when Mr. Fogg and I went in to talk to Mr. Furman, he was busy. He asked us to sit down while he finished a telephone call."

"Yes?" said Benny. "What about that?"

"Mr. Furman kept saying, 'All right, all right, yes, yes.' Then he said, 'I have her telephone number here.'"

"That's all?" Benny asked. "I wonder what that was all about. It's none of my business, I guess. But do you remember the telephone number?"

Henry laughed at Benny. He said, "It is none of your business, but you just want to know everything that is going on. It happens I do remember the telephone number because it was an easy one—222-1212. I'm sure I've seen it near a phone in the store."

Benny thought about the number for a minute. Then he said, "I think I know whose number that is. But I'm not ready to tell you yet. Do you think the call was about ordering something?"

Henry smiled. "I don't think so. It sounded more like a meeting. Something of that sort."

Benny finished his sandwich and bit into an apple. He asked, "What did Mr. Furman say about Mr. Fogg being in the store yesterday after it was closed?"

"Mr. Furman listened to what we each had to say. Then he said, 'I can't tell you the whole story now. But I can say that I'm sure neither of you had anything to do with the lockets.' Then he thanked Mr. Fogg for trying to solve the mystery of the lockets, and he thanked me for being watchful."

"Did you tell Mr. Furman about hearing someone try to put a key in the front door lock?"

"Yes, later in the morning. I told Mr. Furman about the sounds at the door about eleven o'clock last night."

"Wasn't he upset by that?"

"No, he didn't seem to be. He just said quietly, 'I think there was some kind of mistake.' Then he told me not to worry because, after all, nobody had come in."

Benny dropped his apple core into his brown paper bag and looked around for a waste can in the park. He saw a car stopping for a traffic light.

Benny knew that car! It was Grandfather Alden's. Grandfather was driving, but he did not see Benny. Mr. Alden was talking to someone seated beside him.

Benny would have called "Hi!" but the light changed and the car moved away.

There was enough time, though, for Benny to catch a glimpse of the other people in the car, a man and a woman. He was sure the man was Mr. Furman, and he thought the woman was Maggie Douglas. He could not be quite so sure about that.

"What can Miss Douglas, Mr. Furman, and Grandfather be doing?" Benny asked Henry. "Grandfather never said a word about meeting Miss Douglas. And he has heard us talk about her every day at dinnertime."

Henry laughed. "Benny, you know very well you're not the only one in the family who likes a little mystery. Grandfather doesn't tell you about everyone he knows. I'll make a guess. Now I think Mr. Furman's telephone call this morning must have been from Grandfather. He was inviting Mr. Furman to have lunch. That's interesting, isn't it?"

"That telephone number Mr. Furman gave," said Benny. "I'm sure it is Miss Douglas's. I'll tell you how I know. First, Mr. Fogg has it written down on a pad near the phone he uses. And second, it was the phone number in the want ad I answered before we came to Furman's. Remember? Now I know Ted Evans already had the job before I called."

Henry stood up and stretched. Lunchtime was over.

More to himself than to Henry, Benny said, "Now I know how Miss Douglas knew my name and who my grandfather is. That puzzled me when I phoned about the want ad in the paper."

Henry looked at his watch. "Time to get back,"

he said. "You know, this is our last full week to work at Furman's."

"That's right!" Benny exclaimed. "When I'm back in school I'll miss working at the store. I'll even miss Mr. Fogg."

CHAPTER 10

Answers at Last

There was a bulletin board in the store near the lockers where people kept their coats. On Friday morning all the store workers were crowded in front of the bulletin board.

"What's going on?" asked Benny.

Toni said, "Plenty! Next Wednesday afternoon, when the store is closed, everyone is invited to a picnic lunch. You'll never guess where."

"Tell us," Henry said. "We'll never get close enough to the bulletin board to read what's there."

Doris laughed and said, "At Miss Douglas's house! Can you imagine that? Why would she do anything like that?"

"And we're all invited," said one of the salespersons who worked upstairs. "Everyone."

"What do you suppose she'll serve?" somebody else asked. "I'll bet we go home hungry. But I want to go just to see what it's all about."

Even Mr. Fogg read the notice. When Toni asked him if he was going he said he was thinking about it if his back didn't bother him too much.

Henry and Benny told the story of the picnic to Jessie and Violet at dinnertime.

"It just happens we've already been invited," Jessie said. "Grandfather and Violet and me—we've all been asked. We'll be there, too."

Benny turned to Grandfather and said, "Something is going on. And I just don't understand it. I have an idea you know something about this."

Grandfather looked at Benny and said with just a small smile. "I'm having lunch on Wednesday with some old friends. You remember I've known Mr. Furman for years. In fact, I remember when Mr. Furman's father came to the store each day."

"But what about Jessie and Violet?" Benny asked. He looked at his sisters. "I didn't think you knew Miss Douglas that well."

"We met Miss Douglas at Furman's," Jessie said.

"Yes, she helped me buy the blouse I like so much," Violet added.

"There's something else, too," Jessie told her brothers. "Violet and I were at Woodland Path yesterday afternoon."

"And you never told us?" Benny asked. "Jessie, that isn't fair. You've heard us talk and talk about Miss Douglas and how she comes to Furman's all the time."

"Can't we girls have a little mystery of our own?" asked Jessie. "You aren't the only one who can uncover a mystery wherever you go, Benny."

Then Violet looked at the boys' faces and laughed. "I can't be mean to you two," she said. "You won't be able to wait until Wednesday if we don't explain some things."

"We're listening," Henry said. "What's been going on?"

Jessie said, "You know we've been working, too. At the park. You never even once came to swim while I was a life guard there. But it's all right, I know you have been busy. I met some new kids, and one of them knew Benny. He told me how hard you work, Benny—you never have time to talk when you're on the job."

Benny said right away, "I know who that is! It has to be Ted Evans. Right?"

"Right," said Jessie. "Ted likes to know what's going on. He's curious, just like you, Benny. He walked around to see what was happening at the different classes in the park. He stopped to watch Violet's painting class."

"We were painting flowers," Violet explained.

"Anybody can take a class in the park, you know. There were some children painting and a few older people, too."

"Did Ted want to take painting?" Benny asked. He couldn't imagine that.

"No," laughed Violet. "But he said he knew some ladies who might like to paint. And the next day, guess who came? Miss Douglas and her neighbor, Mrs. Fields."

"I remember Mrs. Fields," Benny said. "Ted and I put up the bird feeder for her. She had sprained her ankle."

"That's why she said she wanted to try painting," Violet said. "I was a little afraid to have the ladies in my class. I'm not that good a teacher. But Miss Douglas and Mrs. Fields were so nice that we all had a good time."

"How did Miss Douglas act?" Benny asked. "Was she really pleasant to you?"

"Oh, yes," Violet exclaimed. "She asked Jessie and me to come over to her house after we were through with our work at the park. We knew how to find Woodland Path because Benny had told us so much about getting there."

Jessie said, "Miss Douglas is a lot different in her own home. She's not at all like the woman who goes shopping at Furman's. She told us she had just moved here. She likes Greenfield very much."

"I remembered that Miss Douglas helped me buy my blouse," Violet said. "I asked her how she had learned so much about clothing. She told us she likes to test different fabrics. She washes samples to see if the color runs. She dries them in the sun to see if the colors fade."

Benny said, "Miss Douglas told me she's been testing the different coffeemakers, too."

While the others talked, Henry had been quiet. Now he asked, "But why is Maggie Douglas asking everyone to come to a picnic next Wednesday? It seems like a lot of work just to be friendly."

"You'll have to wait and see," was all Mr. Alden answered when Henry looked at him. And that ended the talk about Miss Douglas, at least for the day.

Benny and Henry were kept busy at the department store. There was a big back-to-school sale, and so Henry was working upstairs in the boys' clothing department.

Benny carried up boxes of sweaters, T-shirts, and socks. He began to think every boy in town was going to have new clothes for school.

On the first floor Benny overheard Mr. Fogg talking to a customer. She had twin boys and wanted to buy them school outfits.

"Try to get Henry Alden to help you," Mr. Fogg said. "He's just working for us this month. But he tries to please his customers."

"Well!" Benny thought to himself. "That doesn't sound like Mr. Fogg at all. Maybe Miss Douglas is right. He growls like a bear, but he isn't so bad when you get to know him."

But Mr. Fogg sounded more like his old self when Benny asked, "Are you coming to the picnic?"

"What makes you ask?" Mr. Fogg answered gruffly. "Who cares if I come? But I guess I'll have to go."

On Tuesday evening, Benny and Henry were talking together about working at the store. Benny was thinking about the picnic. "You know what?" he asked. "I think I know why the picnic is being given. I think the new owner wants to meet all the store people."

"What makes you think that?" asked Henry. "The new owner is in New York. Why would the owner want to come to Greenfield to meet people?"

"The owner is supposed to be in New York," Benny said. "*Supposed* to be. That's the part to remember. But we'll soon see."

When the buzzer sounded for closing time at noon on Wednesday, everyone at Furman's hurried. Soon the dust covers were in place over the counters. Toni closed out her cash register. Salespeople made sure their sales books were in order.

This was the last day of work for Henry and

Benny. August was over. It made the boys feel good when some of their new friends said, "See you next summer. We hope you'll be working with us again."

"I hope so, too," said Benny.

Most of the workers drove or rode with friends, but Benny and Henry rode their bikes to Woodland Path.

It was a beautiful summer afternoon. The first thing the guests saw on arriving was a long picnic table covered with a red-and-white paper cloth. There were paper plates stacked at one end. There were platters with sliced ham and roast beef. There was chicken, too, and cheese and salads. Baskets were filled with rolls and whole wheat bread. It was a feast!

Standing behind the table, ready to help her guests, was Miss Douglas. But she was not the Miss Douglas most of the store people knew. Her hair was fluffy and no longer done up in a tight bun. She wore a red shirt and a denim skirt. Her new earrings looked fine.

"Help yourselves, everyone," she called out happily. "I'm so pleased you could all come!"

Jessie and Violet served iced tea and coffee. They ran back and forth to the house to get more platters of meat and fresh salads. Ted Evans passed the baskets of rolls.

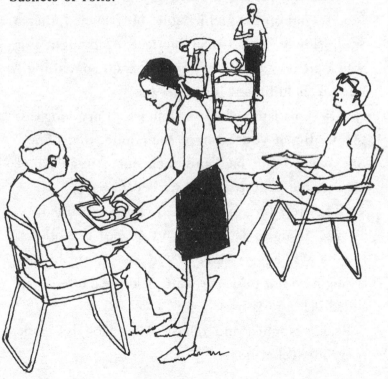

Mr. Furman and Mr. Alden found a shady place
to sit. Doris and Toni sat nearby.

"Is Mr. Fogg coming?" Doris asked.

"There he is now," Toni said. "But what's he
bringing with him?"

Mr. Fogg looked around at the guests and the
food set out on the picnic table. He frowned, then a
smile slowly spread over his face. "I thought this
was a picnic where every guest brings something,"
he said, holding out his paper bag.

"Oh, no," laughed Miss Douglas. "I'm giving this
picnic. But if you brought something, that's fine."
She opened the bag and took out a huge jar of
pickles, the largest anyone had ever seen.

"They're sweet pickles," Mr. Fogg explained.

Miss Douglas laughed, and so did the others.
Maybe Mr. Fogg wasn't exactly sweet, but he was
trying hard not to be the sour pickle he'd often been
called behind his back.

People laughed and talked. Miss Douglas made
everyone feel at home.

After cake and ice cream, Miss Douglas stood up. Someone rapped on a glass, and everyone became quiet.

"Friends," she said, "you all know me as Maggie Douglas. Now it is time to tell you who I really am. I'm—"

"Maggie Douglas Squires!" Benny exclaimed loud enough to be heard clearly. He clapped his hand over his mouth. He hadn't meant to let anyone know he'd solved the mystery.

It didn't make any difference. Maggie Squires laughed and said, "Benny's right, that's who I am. I'm the new owner of Furman's Department Store. I want all of you to know that I'm pleased with the way the store is run."

Some of the guests turned red. They remembered that they had not wanted to wait on this woman. They had found her questions hard to answer and had been rude.

Mr. Furman came over and shook Miss Squires by the hand. He said, "Until a few days ago, I only

knew the name of the owner who had bought
Furman's Department Store. It was M. D. Squires
of New York City. Mr. Alden had assured me this
was a reliable person who had a lot of experience.
He told me the new owner would be fair and not
make sudden changes. I was afraid that might
happen if someone new took over the store."

"Benny, how did you know who I was?" Miss
Maggie Squires asked.

"I just put a lot of clues together," Benny said.
"Those notes about the kind of work people were
doing, you wrote those, didn't you?"

"Yes," nodded Miss Squires.

"And the lockets—you put them on the jewelry
counter."

"Yes, but I really should not have done that," she
said and laughed. "I never dreamed it would cause
so much trouble. And Henry nearly caught me
when I tried to get in the store at night and couldn't
use my key because the lock had been changed."

Sam, the night watchman, was staring at Miss

Squires. "Then I did hear someone in the store," he said. "I just had a feeling I wasn't by myself."

"I was sure you were going to catch me," Miss Squires said. "There wasn't time for me to get out of the store. I didn't know what to do. I stood very still and tried my best to look like a store dummy. I was afraid I'd sneeze or something."

"That was you?" Sam said. "Well, you fooled me!"

Mr. Fogg came up and shook Miss Squires by the hand. "You really do know all about merchandise," he said. "Mr. Furman told us the new owner would know what would sell and what wouldn't. And you really do."

"Why, thank you," said Miss Squires. "I moved to Greenfield a while ago, but I didn't want to take over Furman's Department Store suddenly. I wanted to learn to know Greenfield people and the workers in the store. It wasn't easy to pretend I was cross, complaining, plain Miss Douglas. I want to thank Mr. Furman and all of you for being patient with me. Now we'll all work together and have the best department store anywhere!"

Everyone clapped and one by one came up to greet Miss Squires.

"Benny and Henry, I hope you'll work with us again," Miss Squires said. "Maybe I'll make Benny my store detective."